Jerry Seinfeld
Halloween

Illustrated by James Bennett

To my wonderful wife, Jessica, and our little Sascha, the sweetest candy of all.
—J.S.

To my favorite trick-or-treaters—Susan, Steven, and Brett.
—J.B.

Text copyright © 2002 by Columbus 81 Productions, Inc.
Illustration copyright © 2002 by Columbus 81 Productions, Inc., and
Byron Preiss Visual Publications, Inc.
Audio copyright © 2002 by Columbus 81 Productions, Inc.

Superman created by Jerry Siegel and Joe Shuster. © and ™ DC Comics.
Used with permission.

First Edition

This book has not been endorsed or sponsored by any of the candy companies whose
products are parodied and/or paid homage to in this book.

ISBN 0-316-70625-6

Library of Congress Control Number 2002103231

Printed by Phoenix Color Corporation

Printed in the United States of America

Jerry Seinfeld
Halloween

Illustrated by James Bennett

A Byron Preiss Book

Little, Brown and Company

Boston   New York   London

When you're a kid you can eat amazing amounts of food.
All I ate when I was a kid was candy. Just candy, candy, candy.
And the only really clear thought I had as a kid was *get candy.*

GET CANDY,

GET CANDY,

GET CANDY,

GET CANDY.

Family, friends, school—
they were just *obstacles* in the way
of getting more candy.

So the first time you hear the concept of Halloween when you're a kid, your brain can't even process the idea.

You're like, "What is this? What did you say? Someone's giving out candy? Who's giving out candy?

EVERYONE WE KNOW

is just *giving out* candy?

"I gotta be a part of this!
Take me with you!
I'll do anything they want. . . .
I can wear *that.*

I'll wear anything I have to wear.
I'll do anything I have to do
to get the candy from those
fools who are so stupidly ***giving it away.*** "

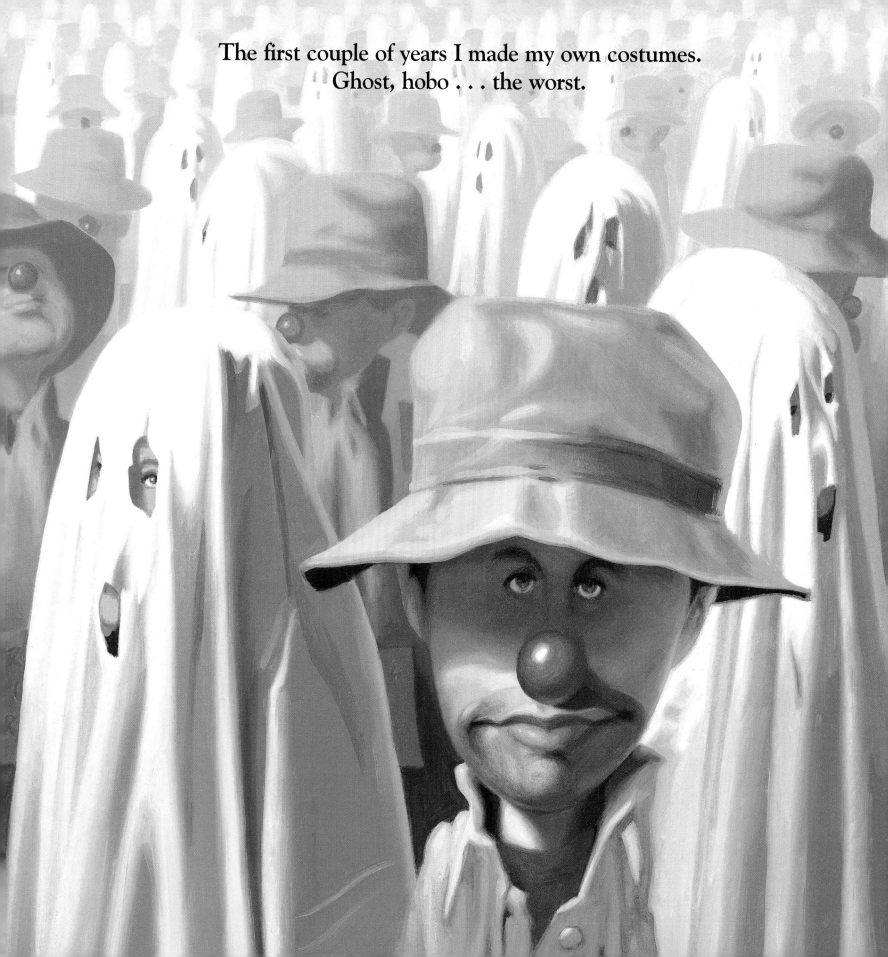

The first couple of years I made my own costumes.
Ghost, hobo . . . the worst.

I knew my destiny was to one day get a real Superman Halloween costume from the store.
You know the one. . . . The cardboard box . . . the cellophane top . . .
mask included in the set . . .

Oh, BABY!

Remember the rubber band on the back of those masks?

That was a quality item. Thinnest gray rubber in the world. It was good for about ten seconds before it snapped out of that cheap little staple they put it in there with. You go to the first house, "Trick or . . . SNAP!
It broke, I don't believe it!

Because when you're little, your whole life is up.
You want to grow up. Everything is up!

"Wait UP!"

"Hold UP!"

"Shut UP!"

"Mom, I'll clean UP. . . .

Just let me stay UP!"

When you're a parent it's just the opposite:
Everything is down.
"Just calm down!"

"Slow **DOWN!**"

"Sit **DOWN!**"

"Come **DOWN** here!"

"Put that **DOWN!**"

"And keep it **DOWN** in there!"

"You're **GROUNDED!**"

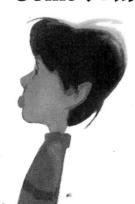
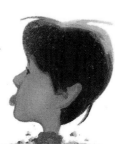

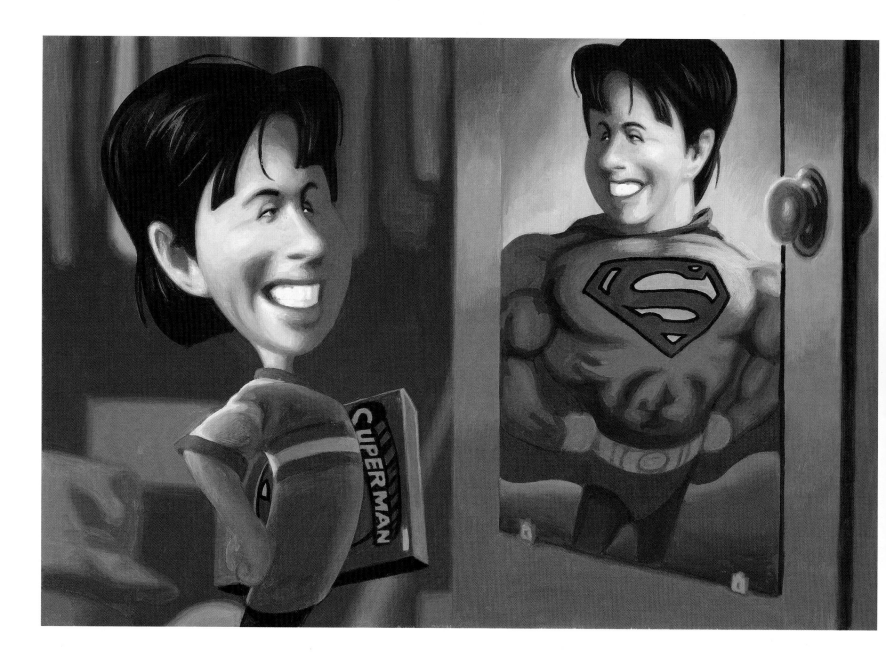

So the day finally came. I finally convinced my parents to buy me an official **Superman** Halloween-store costume.

I was physically ready. I was mentally prepared. And I absolutely believed when I put this costume on that I would look *exactly* like the **Superman** I had come to know on television and in the movies.

Unfortunately, these costumes are not exactly the **super fit** that you are hoping for.

You look more like you're wearing Superman's pajamas.

It's all loose and flowy, the **neckline** comes down to about your stomach.

You got that **flimsy** little ribbon string in the back holding it all together.

Plus my mother makes me wear my **winter coat** over the costume anyway.

I don't recall Superman
wearing a JACKET.
I read every comic book.
I do not remember him ever once
flying with a coat on.
Not like the one I had—
cheap corduroy, phony fur.

So you go out anyway and the mask keeps breaking
the rubber band keeps getting shorter
because you need to keep **retying it.**

It's getting tighter and tighter on your face.
Now you can't even **see!**

You're trying to breathe through that little hole that gets all sweaty.
Whoosh, whoosh.

The mask starts slicing into your eyeballs.
"I can't see, I can't breathe.
But let's keep going.
We gotta get the candy!"

About half an hour into trick-or-treating you take that mask off.

"Oh, the heck with it!"

Year after year, I never gave up on trick-or-treating. But I remember those *last* few Halloweens.

I was getting a little too old for it. . . . I was just kinda going through the motions.

Bing-BONG

"Come on lady, let's go! Halloween, doorbells, candy, let's pick it up in there."

They come to the door; they always ask you the same stupid question. "What are *you* supposed to be?"

"I'm supposed to be *done* by now.
You want to move it along with the 3Musketeers®?

Sometimes people give you the little white bag, twisted on the top.
You know that's gonna be some **CRUMMY** candy.
"No **official Halloween** markings on it?
I don't think so."

"Wait a second, what is this? The orange marshmallow shaped like a big peanut?

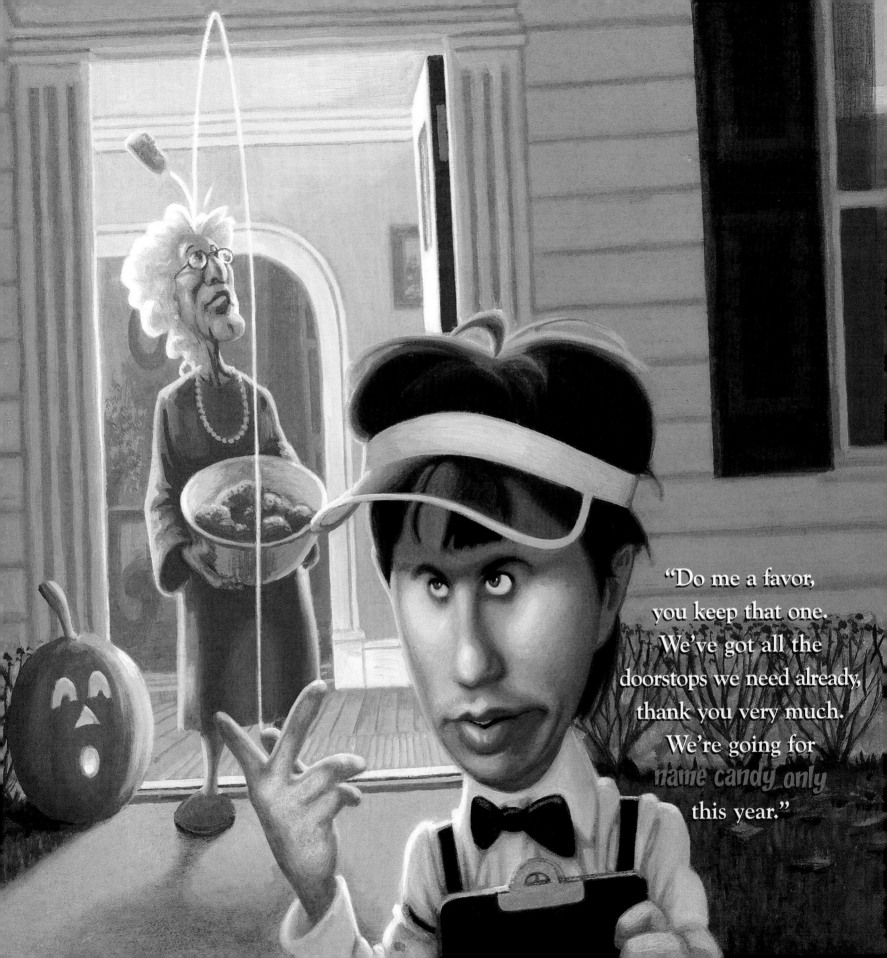

"Do me a favor, you keep that one. We've got all the doorstops we need already, thank you very much. We're going for *name candy only* this year."

At the end of Halloween
I was able to fill a punch bowl
so full of candy that the top
of it would be curved.
It was like a planet.

Next morning, I'd wake up, feel **FanTasTic.**

And that's when I realized, when you're a kid you don't need a costume, you **are** Superman.